It was a beautiful day on the Island of Sodor, and Thomas and Percy were shunting trucks at Brendam Docks. They were being a bit silly, and they accidentally knocked one of the trucks over. A crate fell off, and a suit of armour fell out! Thomas and Percy had never seen a suit of armour before.

"I hope you haven't damaged it," Cranky tutted. Two men checked it over, but it was fine.

"Who does it belong to?" Thomas wondered. But nobody knew. It was a mystery!

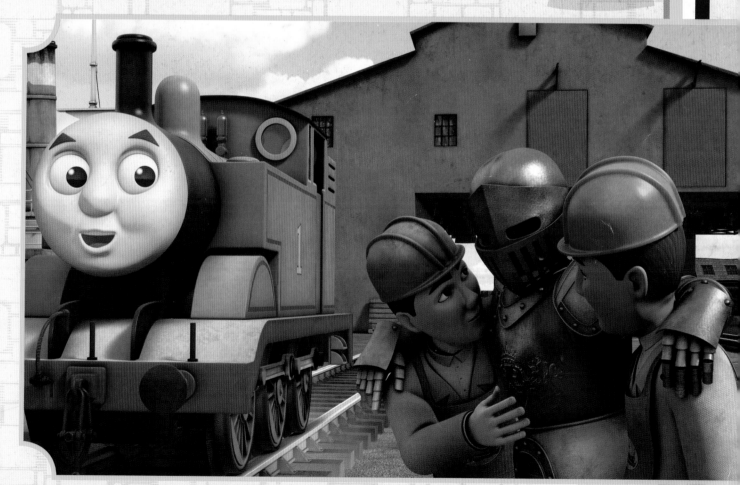

The next day, The Fat Controller told everyone that Spencer was bringing the Earl of Sodor over from the Mainland. Thomas and his friends were sent to the Washdown, then they helped to tidy up Sodor and decorate Knapford Station. Everyone gathered at the station to wait for the Earl. Finally, Spencer arrived and the Earl stepped out of a carriage.

"A celebration? Splendid!" he beamed. "You carry on. I didn't mean to interrupt!"

The Earl got back into Spencer's coach before The Fat Controller could explain that the party was for him!

"I promised Millie I'd be at the estate by two. Enjoy your party!" the Earl said cheerily. And with a wave, he was off. Oh dear! Everybody was very disappointed. And who was Millie?

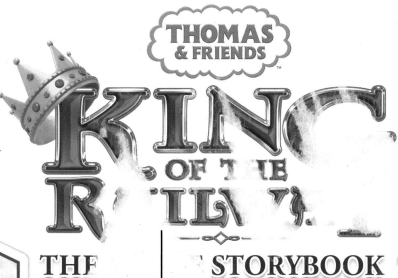

THOMAS & FRIENDS™

KING OF THE RAILWAY

THE | STORYBOOK

Stephen

...pencer

EGMONT
We bring stories to life

First published in Great Britain 2013
by Egmont UK Limited
The Yellow Building
1 Nicholas Road
London W 11 4AN

Thomas the Tank Engine & Friends™

CREATED BY BRITT ALLCROFT

Based on the Railway Series by the Reverend W Awdry
© 2013 Gullane (Thomas) LLC. A HIT Entertainment company.
Thomas the Tank Engine & Friends and Thomas & Friends are
trademarks of Gullane (Thomas) Limited.
Thomas the Tank Engine & Friends and Design is
Reg. U.S. Pat. & Tm. Off.

All rights reserved.

Connor

Millie

HiT entertainment

ISBN 978 1 4052 6724 3
54930/1
Printed in Malaysia

Jack

Caitlin

FSC
www.fsc.org
MIX
Paper from
responsible sources
FSC® C018306

Egmont is passionate about helping to preserve the world's remaining ancient forests.
We only use paper from legal and sustainable forest sources.

This book is made from paper certified by the Forest Stewardship Council® (FSC®),
an organisation dedicated to promoting responsible management of forest resources.
For more information on the FSC, please visit www.fsc.org. To learn more about
Egmont's sustainable paper policy, please visit www.egmont.co.uk/ethical

Stay safe online. Any website addresses listed in this book are correct at the time of
going to print. However, Egmont is not responsible for content hosted by third pa...
Please be aware that online content can be subject to change and websites can co...
content that is unsuitable for children. We advise that all children are supervised wh...
using the internet.

I BN

1 1 0568090 3

1 1 0568090 3

Long ago, before there were any railways, the Island of Sodor was ruled by Kings. The greatest King of Sodor was King Godred. He protected the Island from invaders with the help of his gallant knights-in-armour. They called King Godred's reign a golden age, and King Godred wore a **golden crown**. But one day, the crown was stolen! The thieves were caught, but they refused to say where they'd hidden the crown and it was never seen again.

The ruins of King Godred's Castle can still be found on the Earl of Sodor's estate. These days, instead of knights, it's railway engines who charge about the Island . . .

The next morning, The Fat Controller sent Thomas to the Earl's estate with a special delivery. The mysterious Millie was there to help Thomas unload the crates. Millie was the Earl's engine. She had been stuck in her shed while the Earl had been away which is why nobody had ever seen her. She was very pleased to be out and helping! She jumped forward in excitement and a crate slid off her truck.

It broke open and the suit of armour fell out, **again!**

"**Oh no!**" Thomas wheeshed.

"No harm done," said the Earl.

"This suit of armour is very old and precious but it is also strong."

Thomas and Millie were very relieved.

The workmen sat the suit of armour in Millie's truck, beside the Earl. The Earl put his arm around it to hold it steady – they did look funny!

"If only I had **King Godred's Golden Crown**," sighed the Earl. "That's the one thing missing to complete my surprise."

Millie set off and Thomas was left alone to wonder about the Earl's surprise and the King's golden crown.

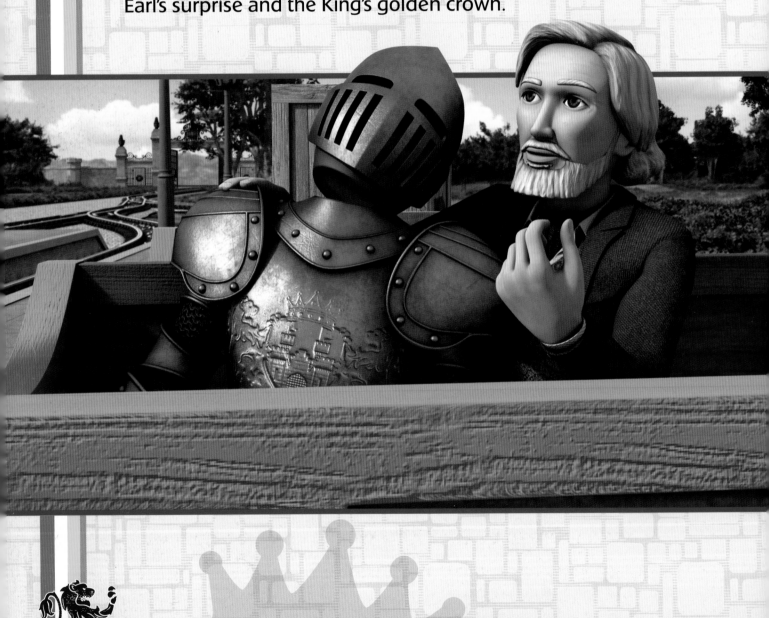

That evening, Spencer came back to Tidmouth Sheds.

"The Earl has borrowed me to act as his private engine!" he told the other engines proudly.

Gordon didn't like Spencer showing off, and the two engines began to argue about who was the fastest.

"Maybe you should have a race!" Percy suggested.

The next morning, Gordon and Spencer raced out of Knapford Station. Spencer set off before anybody said "Go", which Gordon thought was very unfair. He hurried after Spencer, and was just catching up when Spencer pulled off the mainline.

"I'm afraid I have to be **Really Useful** now! Perhaps we can have a proper race another day!" Spencer called.

Back at Knapford Station, Toby arrived with a very important message.

"Henry's broken down!" he told the other engines. "The Fat Controller wants Percy to pull his heavy goods train to the Earl's estate."

Percy was very excited, and he **puffed** off **proudly** to collect the train from Brendam Docks.

At the Docks, Percy met James and Thomas. They'd both been asked to take the heavy goods train to the Earl's estate, too! The three engines began to argue. Then they saw The Fat Controller.

"Please, Sir, who would you like to pull this heavy goods train?" Thomas asked.

The Fat Controller chuckled. "All of you, of course! This train is much too heavy for any of you to pull alone."

So Percy, Thomas and James were coupled to the trucks and off they set for the Earl's estate. When they arrived, they saw new rails, stone and building materials everywhere. Then Thomas spotted his old friend Jack, the front loader.

"I'm helping the Earl – he's restoring Ulfstead Castle!" Jack told Thomas.

"**Fizzling fireboxes!**" Thomas exclaimed. That was exciting news!

Millie arrived with the Earl, and the heavy goods train was split up. Then the Earl spotted a crate with a funnel sticking out of it.

"That crate was meant to go to the Steamworks!" he said.

"What is it, Sir?" Thomas asked. James and Percy were curious too, so the Earl said they could all take it to the Steamworks together, and then he would show them what was inside.

At the Steamworks, Victor was surprised when Thomas, James and Percy arrived.

"What is this thing in a crate that takes so many engines to deliver?" he chuckled.

The Earl jumped down from Thomas' cab with a smile. The engines watched as the crate was lifted off by the crane, and opened to reveal a very old, rusty engine.

"Meet my friend, Stephen!" the Earl smiled.

"I've never seen an engine like you before," Percy gasped. Stephen looked very different from the engines on Sodor.

Stephen smiled. "You mean an engine with woodworm and rust holes? Nobody's seen me in a long time. I haven't turned my wheels in years!"

"We'll have you fixed up in no time!" Victor promised Stephen.

The men hooked Stephen to another train and took him away.

"Sir, why are you rebuilding the castle? And what's inside your crates?" Thomas asked the Earl.

The Earl smiled. "You'll find out soon enough. It's all part of my **big surprise**."

"Is Stephen part of the big surprise, too?" Thomas asked.

"I have a very special job for Stephen. But don't tell him just yet. There's a lot of work to do before he can start."

Thomas promised to keep quiet.

"I have a special job for you, James and Percy too," the Earl added. Thomas couldn't wait to find out what it was.

That night at Tidmouth Sheds, Thomas, Percy and James told the other engines about Stephen. And the next morning they all set off to visit him.

When they arrived, they found Stephen hanging from a crane with his wheels removed. And he was delighted to have visitors! He began to tell them his story.

"I remember when most railways didn't have any engines and the trains were pulled by horses," Stephen told them. "We steam engines were the latest thing and people were worried about us. We didn't always work right!"

"But we soon proved we were stronger and faster than horses. I was lightning fast – they called me '**The Rocket**'! I worked at the mines, and later at the Docks. I could pull four wagons at once! But you new engines are so fast and so strong. That's why I don't work any more!" he chuckled.

Over the next few weeks, Stephen's funnel was straightened, his boiler was repaired and he was given a fresh coat of paint. Finally, Stephen was finished!

"Now you look **Really Useful** again!" Thomas told him.

And it was time for Thomas, Percy and James to go to the Earl's estate to find out what their **special job** was.

"You're so lucky, Thomas," Stephen said sadly. "Being useful is very important!"

Thomas wanted Stephen to be happy. "The Earl has a special job for you, too!" Thomas promised him.

Stephen was **very excited** about his special job. He asked everyone at the Steamworks what it was, but nobody knew. So like a brave knight of old, Stephen set off on a quest to find it!

Stephen went to Brendam Docks, where he met Paxton, Diesel and Cranky.

"I'm looking for my new job!" Stephen told them.

"This is no place for an old engine like you!" Cranky said. Poor Stephen felt disappointed. But if his new job wasn't at Brendam Docks, he'd just have to continue on his quest to find it!

Gordon was hurrying along the mainline when Spencer pulled up alongside him. Spencer raced ahead, and Gordon sped up to catch him.

"Racing again, are we?" Spencer called.

"Yes! And no slipping off onto a siding this time!" Gordon replied. But then Gordon saw Stephen on the track ahead of him. Gordon slammed on his brakes while Spencer raced ahead on the other line.

"I win again!" Spencer jeered. Gordon was **very cross**.

Thomas, Percy and James' special job was to help rebuild the castle roof. The three engines worked together to raise the beams, but it was hard to concentrate because they were so excited. Thomas pulled too far forwards and a roof beam crashed to the ground. Nobody was hurt, but everybody got covered in dust! James was very grumpy, but there was no time to go to the Washdown – they had to carry on with their work or the castle wouldn't be ready in time for the Grand Opening!

At last, the roof was finished.

"I am very proud of you – you all worked marvellously together!" the Earl told the three engines. "Soon everything will be ready for the big surprise."

"I bet I know what it is!" said Percy. "Are you the King of Sodor, Sir?"

"No, Percy. I'm not the King of Sodor," the Earl laughed.

"Then what is the surprise?" Percy asked.

"Come outside, and I'll show you!" the Earl replied.

Outside, Thomas, James and Percy watched as the Earl's crates were unpacked. There were thrones, flags, statues, shields and suits of armour from all over the world!

"I am reopening Ulfstead Castle to the public. Visitors will come to see my collection of medieval treasures!" the Earl said. "The only thing missing is King Godred's Golden Crown."

"Stephen is going to be the Castle Guide!" Millie told Thomas.

"You can tell Stephen about his new job now," the Earl said. Thomas blushed – he shouldn't have told Stephen anything! James steamed off to the Washdown and the Earl asked Thomas and Percy to take away the Troublesome Trucks.

Stephen went to the Blue Mountain Quarry.

"I'm looking for my new job. Could it be here?" he asked Rheneas.

"Are you really strong enough for this kind of work?" Rheneas replied.

"I used to pull four wagons at a time when I worked at the mine! Give me a chance and you'll see!" Stephen replied.

Rheneas agreed, and Stephen was coupled to a long line of trucks loaded with slate. But Stephen wasn't strong enough to pull them forward. The men uncoupled one of the trucks and Stephen tried again, but he still couldn't move them. Finally, Stephen only had one truck left. He managed to get it moving, but as he reached a bend in the track, the truck nearly ran him off the rails!

Skarloey pulled up alongside Stephen. "I don't think there's a job for you here," he said gently.

"The wagons I pulled at the mine were a lot smaller than these!" Stephen chuckled. "Are there any mines around here?"

"There used to be an old mine near Ulfstead Castle ruins," Skarloey told him.

So Stephen set off to find the mine.

Stephen wasn't the only engine feeling slow that day. Gordon and Spencer were on the mainline getting ready for another race when two engines they didn't recognise whooshed past them.

Gordon and Spencer caught up with the engines at a red signal. The new engines were called Connor and Caitlin.

"We've come for the opening of Ulfstead Castle, to bring passengers from the Mainland," Caitlin said.

"We're having a race. Care to join us?" Connor asked. Gordon and Spencer looked uncomfortable.

"No, we're far too busy for racing," Gordon huffed. The signal turned green and Connor and Caitlin sped off. Gordon and Spencer were worried – they might not be the fastest engines on the Island after all!

Stephen went to the mine, but it was boarded up!

"Nobody works here any more," Stephen sighed. "Thomas was wrong – there isn't a job for me anywhere! I'm too old!" He started sadly back up the overgrown track.

Thomas and Percy were pushing the Troublesome Trucks to the Docks. But when they reached a slope on the track, **then there was trouble!**

The heavy trucks started to run away! They dragged Thomas and Percy down the slope, round the castle and onto the overgrown track to the mine.

Stephen saw the Troublesome Trucks fly round the bend towards him! He crashed forward through the wooden boards to get out of the way, knocking his funnel off. A boulder came loose and fell into the mine entrance. Stephen was trapped!

Stephen raced around the mine, but he couldn't find a way out. As he hurried round another bend he bashed into some rocks. When the dust settled, Stephen saw an old wooden chest had split open among the fallen rocks, and there was something shiny inside.

"Wobbling waggons!" he gasped as he saw what it was.

That evening, Thomas went to the Steamworks to find Stephen. Victor told him Stephen had left to look for his new job. Thomas was worried. He looked everywhere for Stephen. Nobody knew where Stephen was, and it was starting to get dark! Thomas went back to Tidmouth Sheds for the night and told the other engines that Stephen was missing.

"He might be in danger!" Thomas wheeshed.

As soon as it was light, Thomas woke all the engines so they could search for Stephen. They hurried out of Tidmouth Sheds and raced along the branch lines, calling Stephen's name. Connor and Caitlin whooshed past them – they were shouting Stephen's name, too!

The engines split up and Thomas went to check the old mine. He spotted Stephen's funnel down below the track, by the entrance to the mine!

"Stephen!" Thomas shouted, blowing his whistle loudly. Inside the mine, Stephen tried to whistle back, but he was very tired from racing round looking for a way out, and he'd almost run out of steam. Thomas was just beginning to think that Stephen wasn't there when he heard a faint whistle from inside.

"Don't worry, Stephen! I'm coming to rescue you! But I need help to move all these rocks!" Thomas peeped.

As quick as his pistons could pump, Thomas hurried to Ulfstead Castle to fetch Jack the front loader, then brought him back to the mine. Jack cleared the entrance and Thomas rushed inside, bravely moving along the weak track as it shifted dangerously beneath him. Then he saw Stephen up ahead.

"Thomas!" Stephen cried. "I thought you'd forgotten me! I'm afraid you were wrong. I'm not **Really Useful** any more," he finished sadly.

"Nonsense!" Thomas replied. "The Earl has a job for you, working on his estate! You're going to show all the guests around. You'll be the Earl's new knight in shining armour!"

Thomas pulled Stephen out of the tunnel to the sound of cheering crowds.

Stephen felt very happy when he saw all the people who had come to see him. He was just going to tell the Earl about the chest he had found when the track suddenly gave way, leaving Stephen hanging off the edge! Any second, Thomas and Stephen could tumble down the steep hillside!

"**Cinders and Ashes**, I'm slipping!" Thomas cried in alarm.

"You need to brace the track!" Stephen shouted.

Jack rushed forward and braced the track with his bucket.

Thomas pulled himself and Stephen back onto solid ground, and everybody cheered again.

"Bravo!" cried the Earl. "Now we must all get ready. Tomorrow is going to be a **very special** day!"

The next day was the opening of Ulfstead Castle. Stephen came out to a special fanfare, proudly pulling some open coaches. And the Earl was in Stephen's cab, wearing the suit of armour! The Earl climbed down and lifted his visor.

"Ladies and gentlemen, engines and coaches," he began. "I'd like to welcome you all to Ulfstead Castle!" The Earl turned to Stephen. "This is my very special steam engine, Stephen!" Thomas, James and Percy whistled proudly.

"Stephen is an expert on history," the Earl continued with a smile. "He'll be more than happy to show you around Ulfstead Castle. And Stephen has found something I thought was lost forever…"

Two men appeared, carrying the old wooden chest Stephen had found in the mine. They set it down in front of the Earl, who opened it and took out a shiny object.

"King Godred's Golden Crown!" the Earl announced, holding it up. Everyone cheered. The top of Stephen's funnel had been painted to look like a golden crown, too! And the Earl had one more surprise to reveal.

"In days of old, the knights of Sodor would race between the Island's castles. Today we will race two of our own shining knights in armour – Connor and Caitlin!" the Earl shouted. Connor and Caitlin rolled forward proudly.

"Spencer and Gordon, why don't you race, too?" Connor called. Gordon and Spencer smiled at each other, then rolled forward to join them.

"Knights in shining armour!" the Earl shouted. "On your marks! Get set!"

"GO!" Connor and Caitlin shouted together. And with that, the four fastest engines raced off across the Island, with all their friends cheering them along.

The End